JAM DAY

by Barbara M. Joosse

pictures by Emily Arnold McCully

Harper & Row, Publishers

Jam Day

 Printed in the United States of America. For information address Harper & Row Junior Books, 10 East 53rd Street, New York, N.Y. 10022. Published simultaneously in Canada by Fitzhenry & Whiteside Limited, Toronto.
Designed by Trish Parcell Watts
10 9 8 7 6 5 4 3 2 1
First Edition

Library of Congress Cataloging-in-Publication Data
Joosse, Barbara.
Jam day.

Summary: An annual family reunion involving berry-picking and jam-making reminds Ben that he is part of a big, noisy family of grandparents, cousins, uncles, and aunts.
[1. Family life—Fiction. 2. Jam—Fiction. 3. Cookery—Fiction] I. McCully, Emily Arnold, ill. II. Title.
PZ7.J7435Jam 1987 [E] 86-46117
ISBN 0-06-023096-7
ISBN 0-06-023097-5 (lib. bdg.)

For Robby,
our Mr. Wonderful

Ben and Mama listen to the whistle of the train and are quiet. Too quiet, Ben thinks.

The other families on the train are noisy. The red-haired boy is crashing toy cars with the red-haired girls. The man with the mustache is laughing

with the lady holding the baby. The baby is saying "mbaa-mbaa."

Ben and Mama are just two.

Ben wishes he were part of a big family. He wishes there were plenty of people and plenty of noise. He wishes there were jokes to share and beds to share and secrets to share.

The train stops.

Mama walks between the people on the train. Ben walks behind Mama, holding on to her skirt.

Ben hasn't seen Grandmam or Grandpap for a long time. What if they don't remember him? What if they aren't happy to see him?

It feels funny off the train, like the sidewalk is moving.

Big, freckled arms sweep Ben off the sidewalk.

"My little Ben," says Grandmam, squeezing Ben tight. Grandmam smells sweet and doughy, like sugar cookies.

"My, my, my," says Grandpap, jiggling the coins in his pocket. He smiles at Ben from under his mustache.

Mama drives the truck, and they all sing "White Coral Bells," Mama's favorite song. Ben sings the loudest because it feels so good to see Grandmam and Grandpap again.

There's a big banner on the front of Grand-mam and Grandpap's house. It says,

WELCOME JEANNIE AND BEN

There are balloons, and lots of relatives running to meet them.

"Here they are," says Aunt Nancy.

"I get to sleep with Ben!" cries Roxie.

"No, me!" cries Petie.

"We can stack up like a sandwich," says Ben, laughing.

The cousins sleep on the floor, under quilts, because there are too many for beds.

During the night Roxie rolls up in the quilt. "Move over, Petie," whispers Ben as he crawls closer to Petie.

Klang-a-klang-a-klang! Grandmam wakes everybody with the bell. "It's Jam Day," she says. "Everybody up."

At FECHTER'S U-PICK 'EM the strawberry plants are in long, neat rows, like braids.

Aunt Nancy sprays everyone's legs with bug spray, for mosquitoes. Grandmam passes out baskets to fill with strawberries.

"One for my basket, and one for me," says Ben, plopping one berry into his basket and one into his mouth. When the juice runs down Ben's fingers, he licks them clean.

"Now weigh your baskets to see how much we picked," says Grandmam.

"We'd better weigh Ben too," says Mama, laughing.

Uncle Louie turns on the radio and listens to the baseball game. "I've never seen such a good year for berries," he says as he hulls the berries.

"You say that every year," says Aunt Nancy. She takes the hulled berries and washes them.

Mama and Ben take turns squashing the berries with a potato masher. Then Grandmam pours the mashed berries, shiny and red, into a big kettle to boil into jam. "Your Mama used to eat so many berries on Jam Day that she got a bellyache," she tells Ben.

"Mama!" says Ben, "you didn't!"

"How many jars are full?" asks Grandpap.
"Where's the wax for the top?" asks Mama.

"Twenty-two jars are full, and the wax is in the middle right-hand drawer," says Grandmam.

"Now," Grandpap says to Ben, winking, "I'm going to teach you my world-famous biscuit recipe."

Grandpap and Ben mix the dough where no one else can see, because Grandpap's world-famous biscuit recipe is a secret. He shows Ben how to pat the dough gently so it will be flaky.

"When I'm home," says Ben, "I'll make some world-famous biscuits for Mama."

When the milky-white biscuits are ready for the oven, Ben says, "Let's add something special. Something red, for Jam Day."

"Red sprinkles?" asks Grandpap.

"Perfect!" says Ben.

Finally, finally Grandmam rings the bell. "Jam's up!" she says, putting out cut-glass dishes of strawberry jam.

Ben passes the world-famous biscuits, special with red sprinkles.

"How lovely," says Aunt Nancy, admiring the sprinkles.

"Yummy," says Roxie, splitting her biscuit and spreading it thick with jam.

"I've never tasted better jam and biscuits," says Uncle Louie.

"You say that every year," says Aunt Nancy.

"Petie took my biscuit!" says Roxie.

"Here," says Ben, passing the biscuits. "There's plenty for everyone."

And there is. There's plenty of jam and plenty of biscuits. There's plenty of people and plenty

of noise. Ben thinks that even the families on the train weren't as noisy as this.

Now Ben knows. He and Mama are not just two. They are part of a big, noisy family with beds to share and jokes to share and secrets to share.

And Jam Day.